MAX'S
JOURNAL

for Cassie and Alexander

MAX'S JOURNAL
(THE ADVENTURES OF
SHARK BOY AND LAVA GIRL)

All designs and illustrations by Alex Toader.
Drawing on page 14 by Josh Brunet.
Drawing on page 100 by Cassie Toader.

A Troublemaker Publishing Book
www.troublemakerstudios.com

First Edition
10 9 8 7 6 5 4 3 2
ISBN: 1-933104-03-1

Manufactured in the United States of America

Special thanks to Robert & Elizabeth
for making this book possible.

I've been HOLDING some curious...

MAX

I started this journal became lately

my own dreams thoughts & other cool dreff AND I need to remember

DREAMS...

my dog SuSu

STORIES i DREAM

april 4th

Last night I had a real
weird dream, I dreamt with
a Shark like creatures
he told me he needs
my help, weird!

← shark
fin on
his
Head.

Profile
– he talked normaly.

I only saw (dreamt) a
profile and everything was
dark.

aprie 5th

again tonight I dream
this creature, he told
me his name

SHARK
BOY!

He has fins all over

he told me again I
have to dream hard and
help him

He has FINS on
ARM ②

He is dressed cooler than
BATMAN... ~~ for some
reason I am not scored
of him, even if he looks
a little bit freaky.
I think he is cool!

WEBS
(how cool is
that?)

— ?

REMINDER : ASK mom for

he rambles on about
How all kids dream in
color and this guy,
s Electric something,
he wants to take the
dreams away, No he
wants to take the
color away from kids
DREAMS I woke up and I
don't remember why?!!

He has
shork
TEETH

maybe tomorrow he will tell me?!!

this stuff for Christmas ⭐ ③

Aprile 6th ⭐⭐⭐⭐

I just woke up and I know I dreamt about the shark boy, he definetly said the electric mister wants to take the color DREAMS OF THE KIDS, — IF KIDS DON4 DREAM in color, they grow up with IMAGINATION... He also said that things are getting worse... AND I NEED TO START TO

BELIVE

HIS EARSHID... HE SAID...

SHOW IT (OR) BRING IT
NEXT TIME

I Just napped and
again Shark Boy showed
up... I am getting Kind
of tired now for a
few nights I keep
Dreaming like this
now even when I nap
after school.

I got to do my homework

Now!

I saw it the ship
Coool!

MOM SAID STOP DAYDREAMING!

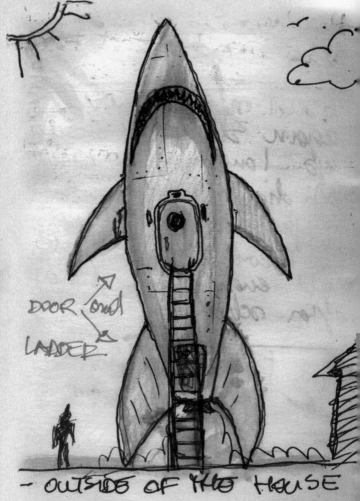

DOOR and
LADDER

- OUTSIDE OF THE HOUSE
- VERY TALL ?

He told me again that I ~~×~~ have to start Believing or we all (KIDS) are in TROUBLE... TODAY APRIL 7TH

BELIVE !

APRIL 7TH late afternoon - Napped again SHARK BOY ~~×~~ Tod me again stuff abart . What we need to do... He also mentioned MINUS and the helpers called SPARK PLUGS he showed me a Hologram of them.

THEY WORK FOR MR. ELECTRIC

APRIL 7TH 11³⁰ pm

I just woke up, I think
I had a nightmare, I am
not sure but Mr. Electri
told me he will crush m
and something happened
a lot of fire and then
he went away, then Shark
Boy showed up and he
said he brought a
⟵ Friend ⟵
I am up now and I
cannot sleep.
mom is downstairs
watching the late show
I hope I will meet the

New friend Odor, I hope is as cool as Sparkbox

I think they are about 3 maybe 4 feet tall

EVIL RED EYES

SPARK PLUG

I think they may be under direct control of my electric. *

THEY FLOAT AND MAKE SPARKS

⑥

dream ... I didn't know why I drew this ... Now it MAKES SENSE

From 3 months ago ... very vague

SHARK BOY
I Drew this AT RECESS AT SCHOOL

NOTE:
when Grandpa gave me this notebook he told me that I will know when to write in it. the time will come he said, you will know when! He was right. He WAS RIGHT

April 8th early entry
I dropped the notebook in a puddle while going to school, I am afraid, pages will not look the same after it DRIES. DRIES almost all pages are wet. ★★★

15

Also today is my
BIRTHDAY I comple
forgot, Shark Boy said tho
I will meet his friend
today. I am debating
in taking a nap
afterschool or wait
centil tonight! Got to Go
class starts...

APRIL 8TH Roccess entry.
I have to wait till toni
to sleep. Mom has a
surprise for me to have,
Grandmother made me
my favorite cake and
she's coming over.

& had another dream
* Shark Boy did NOT
reveal his friend.
but he went on
about places i never
heard of before, like

kids up here

SHARKBOY DOLL

PLANET DROOL

he said that PLANET
DROOL LIES BEYOND THE
MAGELLAN MOONS AND
ALL KIDS GO THERE IN
THEIR DREAMS TO PLAY
AND HAVE FUN.
OH I forgot, PLANET
DROOL is like a BIG
AMUSEMENT PARK WITH
TOYSTORES AND MALLS
AND FERRIS wheels and
Roller coasters EVERYwhere
I Love roller COASTERS!
But I DON'T THINK THIS
PLACE EXISTS, I Looked
IN THE ALMANACH and
THE DICTIONARY AND...

NO PLANET DROOL

PLANET DROOL WHERE
CHILDREN RULE!
(shark boy said that)
DOES NOT EXIST!

I said THAT...

April 10th again last
night Shark Boy rambles
on about Planet Drool
an that, I need to
belive, He mentions
places like Mount
Neverrest and Land of
Milk and Cookies
He's crazy...

9

that's what i think...
he keeps talking about
Giants and a city, a
Boobie TRAP City, very
dangerous! I asked him
about his friend : Shark
Boy said she doesn't
work with NON Believers
ITS A SHE and if I
keep not having
faith in him and
they will look for
someone else soon.
I just noticed he has
5 vents on the side of

his ribs. Just like a shark. [over].

NOTES   MOUNT NEVEREST

MOUNT NEVEREST keeps changing shape and grows and tumbles so must be careful climbing it. ➡

⑩

again checked the dictionary
and almanach also asked
miss BARTON the librarian
about it she said

IT DOES NOT EXIST

How can I believe if
the places Shark Bay
tells me about are
not real

Reminder: Not to write
NEXT TO MY SISTER AT
BREAKFAST

SHE SPILLED MILK
ON MY BOOK

NOTE: THERE IS NOWHERE
I CAN FIND ANYTHING ABOUT
BOOBIETRAP CITY or GIANTS
- YEA IN FABLES →
PLENTY OF KIDS BOOKS
WITH GIANTS. DAUGH!

GROAR

GIANT
←

HAMMER

KID
↓

DOG
↓

COOKiE TREE
OH YEA !!!

⑪

APRIL 11th SHARK BOY
said he'll prove to me
he is real, I just have
to beliice, this mornin
I found a shark Tooth
under my pillow. THIS
is weird

SIDE   RACED
              AROUND IT.
              FRONT

I am finding this prett
unbelievable, but I beliive
now that there is more
to my dreams than
meets the eye.

*THE SHARK TOOTH IS
AN IMPORTANT CLUE*

APRIL 12th MR ELECTRIC
again intimidates
me he tells me not
to belive in SHARK Boy
and his lies.

NOTE* why is there
conflict in my Dream
if its just a dream
why I need to belive
or desbelive...

Curious the nature of
dreams but it's very
QUESTIONABLE THE
ATTITUDE of mr ELECTRIC
and the way he tries
to score me.?????
WHY DOES HE NOT WANT

I am drawing sharks everywhere now

⑫

me to Belive Shork Boy?

XXXXXXX LOVER XXXXXX

why? why? why? why?

*Note to myself : ☆☆☆
NOT TO SCREAM ON THE
SCHOOL BUS "EUREKA
I KNOW THE ANSWER: WHY?

BECAUSE IT'S * TRUE *
ShorkBoy IS TELLING ME
the TRUTH, he is ASKING
for HELP.
I con't wait until
I dream again...

I DO Belive Now

it is very clear to
me now that the
revelations in my
dreams are true
Shark Boy needs
my help and I
am **READY**!

NOTE: mr. Electric
is very full of energy
and Dangerous! *RED EYES*

neon

he can change shape
THE EYES ARE THE SAME ⑬

APRIL 13th Last night

that I belive him r

LAVA GIRL she is

really nice and her

hair is on fire!

she said   that

we must go to the

ICE CASTLE AND help h

get the CRYSTAL ... t

will GUIDE us to the

END of the WORLD and

Beyond to all the

places Shark Boy tol

me about ... ADVENTUR

WILL BEGIN S

APRIL 14th it looks tha
soon we will be read
to embook on a grea
Adenture. Both Shark
Boy and Lava Girl said
to concentrete on my
dreaming... I found a
concentration technique
Book under my Bed
by a CRAZY looking gu
Christopher Brunet...
very interesting, I am
going to read it at
recess time. I can't
wait till the Journe
begins...

APRIL 14th — LATE ENTRY ✳

new revelation about
the CRYSTAL, we must
travel to the ICE
CASTLE, though freezing
snow and blizzards
TO Recuperate the CRYSTAL

XXXXXXXXX OVER XXXXXXX

✳ GUARDED
BY
ICE YETIS?

‑ FLOATING
ICE

‑ CRYSTAL IS
INSIDE

✳ ICE CASTLE..

REMINDER

LAVA GIRL SAID WE h[o]
to KEEP WATCH FOR
ICECLES that FALL &
FOR ICE YETIS,

She and herself alone
must retrive the cryst[a]

the CRYSTAL IS SO COLD WE wo[n]

APRIL 15th — mr Electric showed up in my Dream last night after a 3 day absence. He said he will make me pay for Joyning with the Shark Boy and Lava Girl ... He was glowing Blue angry. A boy about my age was next to him. He said his name is Minus and he will be in Charge of my pain? not to nice, mean...

FREEZE ☆ IMPORTANT ☆

APRIL 16th

Shark Boy told me the story of how he became Shark Boy! It was very cool story... here it goes...

Sometime ago Shark Boy was a normal boy just like me. He used to spend his summers with his dad on a science pod in the Sea of Cortez ... he studied or maybe the INIAN OCEAN?

SHARKS, all kinds of sharks

small ones, big ones and Great White Sharks

RESEARCH POD

The sharks were really cool they got to know him well and they would come around and feed from his hands like cats.

at times he thought
that he understood
what the sharks
were communicating.
he could almost hear
their thoughts.
His father told him
that Sharks don't
think like us...
But Shark Boy
knew different...
One day a big storm
came in... I got to
stop now...
we're going to Mcdonald

[april 17th] - OK! continue from yesterday, I forgot last night to write after *Mcdonald's*. So he told me that a big storm come in and after 2 days, the Research Pod broke apart, Both him and his dad survived But on separate pieces of wreKage... and they drifted apart! that was sad and scary !

... BBQ Burgers... mmm

—

it seems that the
Shark Boy's story is
authentic, I do believe him
as off the wall as
it might sound.

So the Boy survived
on a piece of wrekeg
and then Sharks started
to show up... At first
it looked like they
were going to eat him
but then some of
the sharks that he
used to feed and

Study showed up
and took him to
the safety of the
Shark cove.

there he found all
kinds of things and
later started his
TRANSFORMATION

THE TRANFORMATION
INTO
SHARK
BOY

I will continue
the story tomorrow
now is time to wata

SPY KIDS on

DVD

Yea! we need
some new 3D Glasses.

| April 19th |

very important *

ONLY SHARK BOY CAN TALK WITH - SHARKS -

the boy started growing
gills on each side
then a sharkfin on
his back
then
He ate. nothing but
SUSHI (fresh fish)

* Remind mom !

i keep dreaming of
this getaway dreom
the gang SharkBoy,
LavaGirl and I (max)
need to get away
fast... there is this
contraption like a
SharkBike we ore
on it but it wont
go anywhere !!!
And these things are
After us

I think they look like this

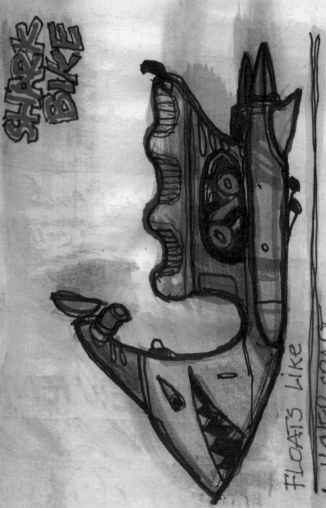

SHARK BIKE

FLOATS LIKE

A HOVER CRAFT

for some reason this
cool Shark Bike won't
GO.... IT FLOATS But
NOT DRIVE... And
I am very scared....

Also Shark Boy and
LavaGirl are very
upset about me
forgeting to dream
something...

I NEED A NEW PEN!

OVER

tell mom about pe

April 21ST

I Keep dreaming about
a place with a
moving sidewalk, I
don't Know if it is
part of Mount Neurest
or Planet Drool but
me and the gang are
Riding on it like
this..

> ## I don't think my dreams are in order

> ## April 22nd

— these Spark Plug
wire things are after
us and Shark Boy
falls in the ocean
only to be shocked by
Electric Eels... very
nasty fishes they are!

april 23rd

I know this is
very strange but
we were riding on
top of the eyes and
mouth of a robot
named TOBOR
that had no body
and we were trying
to catch the train
of thought!

the getaway continue
for ~~some ream~~ some
reason it is none
kind of a cove, a
dream fair. where
Minus and a lizard
sleep with their eye
open... **Weird!** then
I take THIS VERY ou
JOURNAL from them

We could down on
stilts (GIANT)

LIZARD

april 24th

We have to leave fast
We need TRANSPO. out
of here... AFTER we
took the Journal

it is very important
that I dream the
transportation vehicles
all powered up not
like the Shark Bike
fiasco... They all have
gas & keyes..

<u>Same Girl</u> really
loves this Bike the
front wheel hovers
above ground and
it also spews loud
from the pipes,
it goes extremely
☆ **FAST** ☆
it even has wheely
bars just like a
race bike ...
| Very COOL !!!

LAVABIKE for lavaGirl

FLAMES →

wheelie bar

FRONT HOVER
↓

LAVA ENGINE

Lava Bike specifications

ENGINE: V-2 LAVA POWER PLANT WITH 1000 HP

1000 Horse Power

FUEL: LAVA FUEL

* EXTRA HOT OCT. *

TRANSMISSION: DUAL

primaries provides pow
VIA: 2 chains to rear
wheel: DUNLOOP 250m

6 speed automatic
(FLEX-O-MATIC)

TANK & FRAME BUILT BY
Jesse Jameson ESQ.

[May 2nd]

I know there are
missing pages but
from April 25 to
May 1st (yesterday)
I didn't dream anything
or I do not remeber
" I was really sick
with mello fever...
" so I either do not
remember any dreams
or the cold medicine
took them away..

New Dreams ⟹

SharkBoy has his own vehicle:

A SharkBoat with Turbo chargers!!!!

it is the coolest powerboat I ever dreamt of...

it has 2 Turbo charger Jet engines on its sides and has fins Shark fins. also it looks very

FAST ➡️

SHARK

HOVER BOAT with

Turbochargers...

Just like for a Girl
Shark Boy really
loves his Shark
Haer Boot with
TurboChargers....
it looks like it
was made just
for him....

HAPPY
Shark
Boy

REVELATION

everything that we
need to finish the
quest on Planet Drool
it will be revealed to
me in my dreams
also I have to write
everything down
(it is very important)
I must not leave out
any details or we
could Be DOOMED.
I must make sure the
journal is safe and →

Must Never , let
Aqua Girl touch
it she can burn
it to a crisp if
she touch is it.
must remember to
tell her that.
Aqua Girl must
never touch this
journal ✳

IMPORTANT

the strangest dream
about the ice castle
and Lava Girl
trying to cross the
ice bridge with Shark
Boy and I. but she
will melt the
bridge with her
lava power....
So Shark Boy and
I started to think
how can she cross
it.....THINK...THINK

ICE GUARDS

ICE

May 4th ⭐

it came to me!!

dar Girl must

SLEEP WALK

OVER THE

BRIDGE

I MUST REMEMBER

TO TELL HER

is

IMPRTANT

46

that is the only
way we will
not melt the ice

That is the only
way we all can
Get to the Ice
Castle.

(47)

POWER CORDS

must stay away
from power cords
they are very
Dangerous

They are every
corner we turn
they try to

SHOCK

us...

(48)

Just like the

Electric EELs...

49

May 5th ☆ ☆ ☆ ☆

We are in the ⑤⓪
graveyard of
Dreams... it looks
very scary and that's
where we meet
TOBOR the ROBOT.
But the only things
that work are
his Eyes and mouth

nice guy

this is a more clear drawn
than the one I had before...

we ride on
TOBOR we
need to catch
the train of

In order to get to the Ice castle we need to ride the **Train of Thought** there. But first we need **Tobor's** help to catch the train... Tobor is very helpfull and fast he flies like the wind...

Thought...

May 6th

the train of
thought is a
bunch of school
buses chained
togheter and it's
going very,
very fast, Tobor
droped us off...
on it

May 7th

Planet Drool ?!

I finally ~~dreamt~~ had a dream where I know how we landed on the planet.

We Chrashed

MAY 8th ✳ ✳ ✳

WRONG!

the train of thought doesn't take us to the ice castle it CRASHES INTO THE LAND OF MILK & cookies, I had a dream last night very CLEAR ➤

this is like a big changing puzzle of Dreams that I have to remember and put toghether... :)

MAY 9th

the land of milk and Cookies is very weird, full of cookies and ice cream mountains, and chocholate cookie trees and a river of 56 Milk (warm milk)

I dream that I was sleeping on a giant cookie and SharkBoy was playing a cookie Guitar ... and white chocolate dolphins ~~were~~ were singing and Lava Girl was getting angry ... and the Cookie is SINKING in milk

May 10th

a bad dream where
we (Shark Boy,)
LavaGirl and I)
are fighting
HAND to HAND
power cords & plugs.

IT's an ARMY of plugs

Shark Boy

has the power to summon oce animals ... He calls in The fighting fish army ...

Fighting Fish

dream not complete... I woke up

May 11th it looks

that we are saved

by one of my

dreams but not

quite. I dream

of a Banana

Split Boat that

we can sail to

safety .. it is

a Catamaron

made of bananas

and ice cream

we control it
with the cherry
stem ... it's cool
maybe we can
eat it et the eve

the Banana Spli
rides on the
stream of consciou
that is the true
way to the ICE
CASTLE & the Crystal
61 Heart ⭐⭐⭐⭐

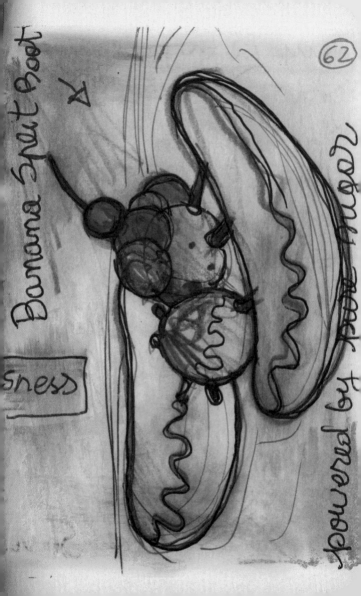

May 12 th early

entry.... I beleive

that we walk into

a TRAP and

MINUS captures

us... also we end

up in a Dungeon

we are all locked

up... Then the

La Lu's show up

again. Their

ringing makes Shar

63

that is how we
got out of the
Dungeon.

Shark Boey ate
through the bars
he ripped through
every bar and
shackle. Everythi
was in shreds..

We escaped the
⑤ DUNGEON!!!

May 15th

the mind Game.

revelation is extraordinary. I never thought such mind puzzles exist or could be invented. I (we) are lucky to have played so many games. IT comes handy. WE CAN DO IT

◁△△ May 16th

~~Lava Girl was wrong!~~
today I got
a good look
inside of the
ICE CASTLE.
it is full of
ice sculptures
of ~~real~~ people
FROZEN... SOLID!
the ice crystal
is atop a thin
icicle about 10
story high...
⑥⑦ IT'S BRIGHT !!

It's Shark Boy that takes the lead
It's Shark Boy that takes the lead

ONLY SHARK BOY
can get it, he
has CLAWS and he
can climb.

ICE CRYSTA

68

IMPORTANT

the shark Rocket must be started by Kicking the control panel. AFTER THE main control box appears. PUSH GO to go and Push STOP to stop. the ship (Rocket) is always on AUTOPILOT

69 REMEMBER

May 18th

the Roller Coaster on mount NeverRest is not what is seems it Never stops...
and a lot of kids are scared. the Mountain is full of caves and it seems it con change. the Roller Coaster is very Fast. We need to STOP it!!! ...

May 19th

A very cool dream!
last night I meet
the **ICE PRINCESS**
at the **ICE CASTLE**

She is very
BEAUTIFUL and
She looks a lot
like **MARISSA**. from my class

(88) what is   ◁—? this ???

FOR another * unknown reason I had a dream about **RACING** across the FROZEN OCEAN and then every thing turns Dark **AS** if **Mr. Electric** has shut down the whole Planet. I (we) wonder if he has such power... Could it Be POSSIBLE?

May 21st

Lava Girl gets FROZEN... for good

I must tell her not to touch the crystal ... I must Remember****

73

FROZEN LAVAGIRL

74

May 22nd

LAVA
GIRL'S
Home ↙

the Volcano is the answer we are looking for!!!

the VOLCANO will SAVE her (Lava Girl)

(75) [May 25th] why?

why is Lava Girl
giving us to
eat: [LAVA Rocks]

I don't Know what
Kind of nose Shark Boy
Has but the Sushi
he is passing around
is not to good!

Lava Girl keeps
asking questions
about her identity,
and every time,
I have the same
problem: **I DON'T
KNOW what to
tell her...**
She definetly has
a conflict within
her.

best sushi

STINKS

May 24th | important

no Distractions

Shark Boy contin
to tell me how
to concentrate on
my dreams.
If i don't we
could be lost in
the Sea of Drea

NO DISTRACTION

① concentrate!

May 28th) Revelation

Tobor has a
s clue for us
that I am writing
down * (must remember)

The secret is in
your dreams.
(my)

and that we
s most not stop
in the Graveyard of
: Dreams for Too long

NIGHTMARES

78

"Mr Electric •
NO DREAMING"

He dreams that is bad ...

mr. Electric

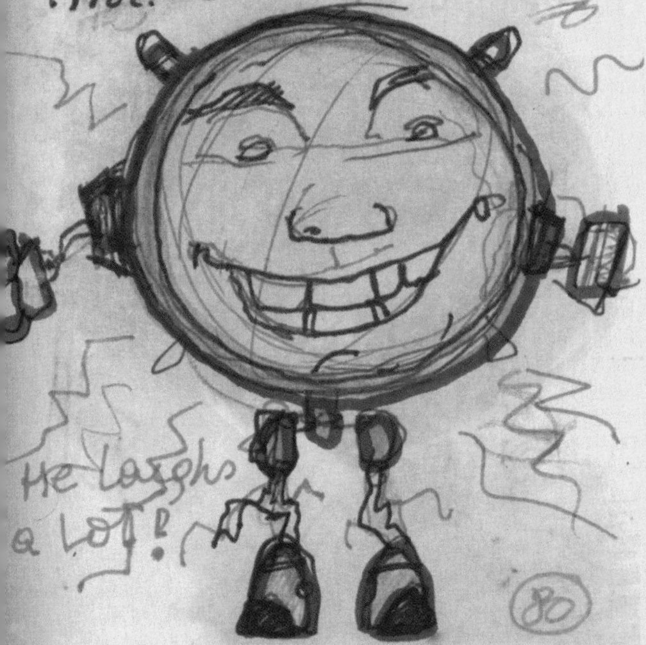

for some unknown
reason the following
words resonate in
my mind:

☆ ☆ ☆ ☆

DREAMS KEEP YOU
FROM SEEING WHAT
RIGHT HERE IN FRON
OF YOU.

mr Electric can
send his arm far
away.

mr Electric's Cord hound

82

made out of electrical cords (very loud)

they bark!

1000

(83)

ANTENNA

ROBOTIC
3 FINGER
ARM

PLASMA

Mr. Electric Detail

BULBS

2 PRONG
CLAW

Very high
Voltage plasma

LEGS

May 29th
mom and dad why
Do I dream this
Mom
Dad
I am not too good at drawing people

May 30th

the usual dreams
become more intense
they are also clearer

AND i Remember
MORE !!!

Some of the adventures
are very dangerous!
Mother and father
will not approve
of the stuff....

⑧⑤ maybe if they knew

[* Note] - Lava girl does not use her power of fire all the time ... only if we are in donger

she con really figh

also she keeps asking who is she? why she is like that?

questions that I do not know how to
(87) answer ... for now!

WATER BANDS

shark suit

Shark Boy

new drawing based on better dream

| HINT | LOCATION OF PLANET
☆ DROOL ☆

I woke up and I keep
repeating a poem:

BEYOND THE MOONS OF MAGELLAN
IN A PLACE AS FAR AS IT SEEMS
ACROSS A SEA OF STARS
AND 9 SEAS OF DREAMS,
IT IS NOT TOO FAR
AND IT IS NOT TO CLOSE
IT COULD BE AS FAR
AS THE TIP OF YOUR NOSE

IT'S A PLANET OF FUN
WHERE ALL THE KIDS RULE
IT'S A DAY DREAMERS PLACE
IT'S CALLED PLANET DROOL!

(89) WHY I AM DREAMIN
OF IT NOW???

May 31st

The Hint poem still
resonates in my
head ... How and why
I need the secret
location if I am
~~stoned~~ already there
in my dreams ...

Maybe there is a
Reason

Maybe i have to
tell Shark Boy and
Lava Girl no they
can always come
back to Planet
DROOL ?

(we will (shall) see)

90

April 1ˢᵗ | Today is
not going to be
a good day of
school, I know.
I will be made fun
of... But maybe
I can tell them
about my Dreams?

I hope I do not run
into LINUS TODAY.

**TOBOR TELLS ME TO
DREAM BETTER
DREAMS !?!**

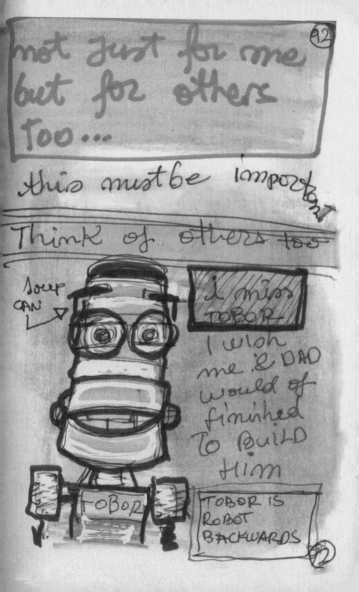

April 2nd

I was right abut yesterday. Lines picked on me all day yesterday 🙁

BUT new things were revealed ~~to~~ to me : WE HAVE TO TAKE OR RIDE THE TRAIN OF THOUGHT to the LAND OF MILK an COOKIES ... which we must CROSS in the BANANA BOAT?

93

this is confusing
I dreamt before that
we were on a cookie
that is sinking

YES

THIS IS A HARD WORD TO SPELL

OR IS IT THE STREAM OF CONSCIOUSNESS THAT WE ARE RIDING??

THE STREAM OF
CONSCIOUSNESS?

IT IS CLEAR NOW
WE DEFINETLY
RIDE THE
BANANA BOAT ON
THE STREAM
OF CONSCIOUSNESS

me

ELECTRIC IS BACK!
He must not be
allowed to freeze the
PLANET. He will BE
completely in charge!

Shark Boy
does not like the
La La's singing it
sends him in a
rage. (SHARK FRENZY)

April 3rd

mad mark

86

April 4th

IT IS A VERY CLEAR
DREAM

we must sneak into
MINUS' LAIR and take
back my Dream Journal
this very Journal. ☆

IMPORTANT ! ☆

the Journal is
the
ANSWER TO ↓

㉗ my questions in
on DREAMLAND...

April 5th

WATER is not good for **LAVA GIRL** "she does not like WATER"

WATER CAN MAKE LAVA GIRL FIZZLE out ✳

I wonder if something BAD is going to happen because I dREAMt of LAVA GIRL AND SHARKBoy LifeLESS on the Shore of the SEA OF Confusion

SLEEPING?

i finally told April 6
someone else about my
dreams. Cassie is one
of my classmates one
she belives me.
At recess she drew me
a picture of LaVa Gi
i had to put it here

Finally Someone
belives me - YEAH!

Cassie is cool and
pretty good artist too

Corsie Drew this
LAVA GIRL

60

April 7

I had a really cool dream last night... TOBOR told me that if i keep dreaming the right dreams, for all the right reasons, EVERYTHING WILL WORK out, and Dreams will come TRUE

(101)

YOUR DREAMS GO HERE →

make sure to write them down

name: ____________
____
____

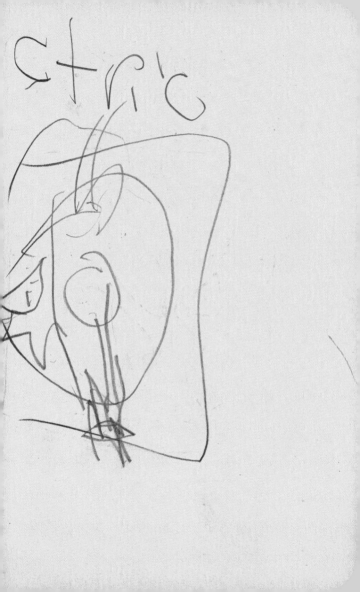

Royal Au

At Stitches

Phantom

King Pariah

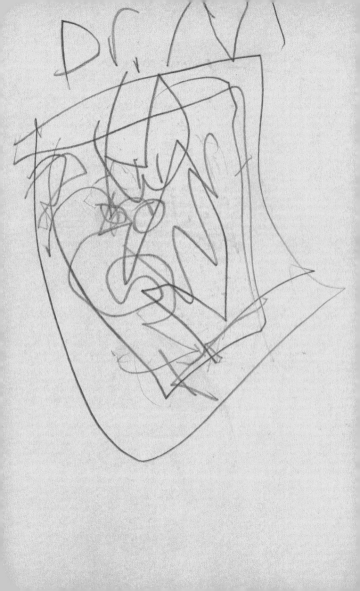

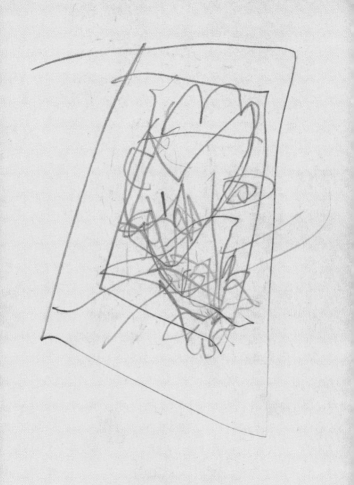

Faerie

Marathon

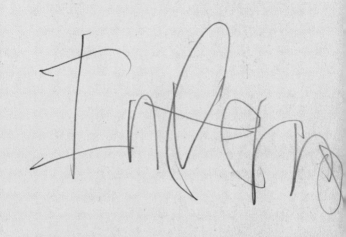